SUPER SISTER

Gwyneth Rees is half Welsh and half English and grew up in Scotland. She went to Glasgow University and qualified as a doctor in 1990. She is a child and adolescent psychiatrist but has now stopped practising so that she can write full-time. She is the author of many bestselling books, including the Fairies series, the Cosmo series and the Marietta's Magic Dress Shop series, as well as several books for older readers. She lives near London with her husband, Robert, their daughters, Eliza and Lottie, and their cat, Magnus.

Visit www.gwynethrees.com

Gwyneth Rees

MY SUPER SISTER

Illustrated by Ella Okstad

MACMILLAN CHILDREN'S BOOKS

First published 2012 by Macmillan Children's Books
a division of Macmillan Publishers Limited
20 New Wharf Road, London N1 9RR
Basingstoke and Oxford
Associated companies throughout the world
www.panmacmillan.com

ISBN 978-0-230-76755-3 (HB)
ISBN 978-0-330-46114-6 (PB)

3 5 7 9 8 6 4 2

A CIP catalogue record for this book is available from
the British Library.

Printed and bound by CPI Group (UK) Ltd, Croydon CR0 4YY

For Eliza and Lottie

EMMA

MEET THE

SAFFIE

MUM

DAD

CHARACTERS

GRANNY

DOROTHY & ELVIRA
Saffie's dolls

HOWARD

CEDRIC

CHAPTER 1

My name is Emma, and I live with my
perfectly ordinary mum Marsha, my
perfectly ordinary dad Jim and my six-
year-old sister Saffie.

Saffie and I both *look* ordinary enough –
though if you met us you probably wouldn't
guess that we're sisters. I have straight dark
brown hair with brown eyes, whereas Saffie
has extremely curly reddish-brown hair and
blue eyes. I'm tall for my age, whereas Saffie
is short for hers. I'm quite shy with people
I don't know very well, whereas Saffie will
chatter away to anyone.

But despite being different in many ways,
we do have one very important thing in
common . . .

You see we both have the same
superpower!

It's not that Saffie and I can fly, or make
ourselves invisible, or read minds, or make
our bodies incredibly elastic or anything
amazing like that. But what we *can* do is
make all sorts of non-living objects come to

life – which Mum says is called *animation*.
This weird gift runs through my mum's side
of the family but it always skips a generation,
which is why it missed out Mum and
jumped straight from Granny to us.

So now you're probably thinking, Wow!
Having a superpower must be really cool!
Well, it is in lots of ways . . . I mean, Saffie
and I can do loads of extraordinary things
that our friends can't. For instance, Saffie can
make her dolls *really* talk to her – not just
pretend talking. And I can make my pencils
dance all over the desk if I get bored while
I'm doing my homework. And we can have
lots of fun with all Granny's garden gnomes!

But it isn't all fun and games. Dad is totally
freaked out by our 'unnatural ability', as he
calls it. It gets a bit irritating after a while,
the way he just can't seem to get used to the

idea. I mean, he *still* nearly jumps out of his skin every time one of his shoes says hello to him when he goes to put it on. And then there's Mum, who you'd think would be pretty cool about the whole thing, wouldn't you? After all, she grew up in a house where the vacuum cleaner did the cleaning all on its own, the washing always hung itself out on the line to dry, and her toothbrush used to come and find her if she forgot to brush her teeth. But Mum says she hated having to live side by side with all those crazy objects that Granny had brought alive, especially as she had no control over them herself.

So anyway, Mum is just as stressed about our special powers as Dad is, and not just because she doesn't want to have to share her house all over again with a bunch of dancing brooms and out-of-control cutlery.

She's also scared because she says that some people out there might want to take Saffie and me away and do lots of clever scientific tests on us if they find out about our powers.

Granny is always telling Mum to stop worrying so much. 'After all, nobody has turned them over to the local science laboratory yet, have they? And it isn't as if your neighbours haven't *already* witnessed a few odd things . . .'

Mum had to admit that Granny was right. You see, although Saffie and I are absolutely *not* allowed to use our superpowers outside the house, there are times when it just sort of happens – especially when Saffie is upset about something.

But then something changed that meant even Granny had to agree that we totally *should* start worrying . . .

★

It was a Saturday at the start of the
summer holidays when our new next-door
neighbours moved in.

That afternoon Mum sat Saffie and
me down together and spoke to us very
solemnly. 'I want you two to be very careful
around our new neighbours. We don't
know what they're like, and remember . . .
when it comes to your special ability, we
can't trust *anybody*.'

'Yes, Mum . . . I know . . .' I said with
a yawn, because, like I said before, our
mother stresses all the time about other
people finding out about us.

Saffie looked like she was hardly even
listening. Her best friend, Rosie, had lived
next door, and Saffie was so upset and cross
about her moving away that she'd refused to

say a proper goodbye or to stand outside and wave nicely with Mum and me as they'd driven off.

As soon as Mum had finished talking to us my sister muttered, 'Don't *care* about the new neighbours!' in a silly baby voice. Then she stomped upstairs and shut herself in her bedroom, where she started to play a very angry game with her dolls. It sounded as if they were calling each other names and throwing things at each other. It's weird, but it seems that when Saffie's in a bad mood everything she animates is in a bad mood too.

'Oh dear. I suppose we'd better check nothing's getting damaged up there,' Mum said with a sigh. I knew before she even said it what was coming next. 'You go, Emma. You're always so good with the dolls. If I go up there I'll lose my temper with them and it will only make things worse.'

I let out a big sigh too and put on my grumpiest face. 'Oh, Mum, do I *have* to?'

Mum got firm with me then and called me by my proper name, which I hate. 'Yes, Emmeline, you do. As I've told you many times before you are the best equipped to deal with your sister when she gets like this. I wish that wasn't the case, but it is. So please just go up there and see what you can do! And don't let that red-haired rag doll get the better of you – she's always the troublemaker!'

I trudged up the stairs, feeling cross.

'Serafina, what are you *doing*?' I demanded angrily as I pushed open her bedroom door. If Mum was going to call *me* by my proper name then I didn't see why I shouldn't call Saffie by *hers*. (Too late I remembered that

8

lately my sister had started to absolutely love her name because she thinks it makes her sound like a very exotic princess.)

My sister didn't reply.

Inside her bedroom her two favourite dolls, Dorothy and Elvira, were squabbling with each other. Dorothy is a very cheeky-looking rag doll with brown freckles and long red woollen hair, and Elvira is an old

hand-me-down dolly that was our mum's when she was a girl. Elvira has a soft lumpy body and a delicate china head, and Mum is always really protective of her. If you ask me, that's why Mum is so bad at handling any fights between Saffie's dolls, because she always takes Elvira's side no matter what.

Elvira was the first object Saffie ever brought to life after Granny discovered a box of Mum's old toys in the loft when we were staying with her one time. Mum actually cried when Elvira stood up and smiled at her, partly because it was the first time Saffie had used her gift and partly because Mum suddenly remembered how much she had loved it when Granny had brought Elvira to life for her as a child. (She said she'd almost forgotten that there had been some *good* things about having a mum with a superpower.)

In Saffie's bedroom the floor around the two dolls was littered with smaller toys that had clearly been used as missiles. An entire dollies' tea-set was scattered about the room and there were books everywhere.

'I don't care if I never see you again, Miss *Straw-for-Brains*!' snapped Elvira rudely.

'My brains are made from the best quality stuffing!' Dorothy defended herself. 'And at least *my* head isn't hollow like yours. If your head ever gets cracked then we'll all be able to look inside and see that you haven't got any kind of brain at all!'

'Elvira! Dorothy!' I said sternly, but they ignored me.

Saffie was lying on her bed with a face like thunder. 'Go away!' she grunted at me without taking her eyes off the dolls.

I decided to try a different approach.

I chose the teddy bear that was sitting on Saffie's window ledge. His name is Howard and he's a sensible brown bear dressed in red dungarees and a little bow tie. Toys tend to have their own personalities (as well as being influenced by whoever brings them to life), and the more a toy gets animated then the stronger its personality becomes.

Howard used to be mine, which Mum says is the reason he's so level-headed. He's *always* sensible – even when Saffie threatens to de-animate him if he doesn't let his hair down. In fact, once, when Saffie brought him to life and gave him some rice to throw down at Dad (who was mowing the lawn), he told her she was very silly and actually refused to do it.

I knew he was the perfect choice for what I had in mind.

This is the bit that's difficult to describe – what it actually feels like when you make something come alive. All I can say is that it doesn't hurt, it doesn't feel unnatural, and when I was little I couldn't understand why everyone else couldn't do it too. It's really just a case of looking at an object and then sort of mentally *zapping* it into life. Of course the *zapping* is the bit that's difficult to describe. Granny says it uses a very special part of our brains, a part that just doesn't function that way in normal humans. (Dad calls it the *wacky* part, though not in front of Granny.)

As I focused really hard on Saffie's teddy I felt that funny 'ping' inside my head, and the next moment he was folding his arms together and glaring severely at both dolls. 'Cut it out, both of you!' he growled in a voice that made them jump. He stayed standing on the window ledge as he addressed Saffie sternly. 'Now just you listen to me, young lady . . . We all know how upset you are about Rosie moving away,

but she's only moved to
the other side of town.
You'll still be able to
see her.'

Saffie looked at me
rather than her teddy
as she replied, 'But we
won't be able to visit
each other without
a grown-up and we
won't be able to play
in our special den any

more.' She and Rosie had converted the old
garden shed in Rosie's garden into a den,
and they used to spend hours playing there
together.

I did feel sorry for her then because I
knew how much she loved that den.

'Maybe the new family will have children

too,' I said in an attempt to cheer her up. Rosie's mum hadn't known if they did or not – in fact she'd hardly known anything at all about the people who were buying her house. Dad says that's quite unusual. (Dad is an estate agent and he'd been a bit miffed that Rosie's parents hadn't asked *him* to sell their house so that he could personally vet our new neighbours.)

'I don't care if they *do* have children,' Saffie declared huffily.

'Well, you should. They might let you play in their shed with them if you ask them nicely.'

'It's not up to them,' my sister said angrily. 'That shed is Rosie's and mine. It's our secret den and no one else is allowed inside unless *we* say so.'

'Don't be silly,' I said, starting to get

impatient. 'Listen. The new people are moving in this afternoon. I'm going round to say hello to them later with Mum. Why don't you come too?'

But my little sister just narrowed her eyes and stubbornly shook her head. She can be very, *very* stubborn when she wants to be. 'I *told* Rosie I didn't want her to move away,' she declared, at which point Elvira lunged at Dorothy and gave her long woolly hair a sharp tug.

Dorothy yelped but immediately recovered enough to grab a teacup to hurl at Elvira, who had climbed on to Saffie's beanbag chair, then up on to the window ledge to hide behind Howard. Just as Dorothy hurled the cup at her, Howard ducked and the cup hit Elvira smack in the face. Elvira started wailing and I rushed over to the window ledge to pick her up before Mum heard.

That's when I looked out of the window and spotted a boy my own age in the neighbouring garden, staring up at us. And judging by the look of disbelief on his face I was pretty sure he'd seen everything.

CHAPTER 2

I quickly leaned out of the window and
called down to him, realizing he must be our
new neighbour. 'Hi! We were just having
a . . . a . . .'

Lying to protect Saffie or myself is
something Mum has given me permission
to do and usually I'm pretty good at it. But
right then I couldn't think of anything. My
mind seemed to have gone blank.

'. . . puppet show!' Saffie rescued me as
she came over to see who I was talking to.

'Pretty crazy puppet show if you ask me!'

the boy called back, grinning. 'Still . . . girls are always playing babyish pretend games with their dolls.'

We watched the boy – who was blond and skinny – disappear round the side of his house.

Saffie and I immediately scuttled across to our parents' room, which faces the street. Out of the window we saw the boy emerge from the side path, dodge past the bins, which Rosie's family had left out the front, and walk over to a car that was parked outside. The car hadn't been there the last time I'd looked.

The boy opened the back passenger door and took out a Spiderman rucksack, poking out of the top of which was a scruffy-looking toy bear.

I turned to look at my sister, who seemed

to be concentrating very hard as she gazed
in the direction of the boy and his bear.
'Saffie . . .' I began tensely. 'You're not
trying to—'

I broke off abruptly as the teddy bear
suddenly gave his head a little shake, then
wriggled out of the rucksack and leaped to
the ground without the boy even noticing.

'Saffie, no!' I scolded her. But the bear was already marching across the drive, swinging its stumpy paws and heading for the bins.

'He shouldn't have called us babyish,' Saffie said with a grin as we watched the bear climb inside.

Not long after that a huge removal van arrived and Saffie and I sat at the living-room window watching it being unloaded. We also got a quick glimpse of a couple who looked around the same age as our mum and dad, but we didn't see the boy again. I knew I had to do something about that teddy bear, but as the bin men weren't due until Tuesday – and it was only Saturday – I reckoned I had plenty of time.

Mum seemed to have temporarily lost

interest in our new neighbours because she and Dad were too busy arguing about Granny. Dad always creates a huge fuss whenever Mum wants to invite Granny to stay. Dad says that not only is Granny the most annoying mother-in-law anyone ever had, but it's all her fault that Saffie and I have turned out to have these weird powers.

'That's just not fair, Jim,' Mum is always saying – and was saying again now. 'It's not *her* fault that one of her ancestors got accidently struck by lightning and had their DNA altered, is it?'

Dad just rolled his eyes as if he thought the story that's been handed down in our family about how our 'gift' originated was highly unlikely in any case.

Mum sighed. 'Jim, she *has* to come and stay with us. She's the *only* one who can teach Saffie how to control her power so that she can start school.' (Mum was homeschooling Saffie, which she said had made her hair start to go grey.)

'Why can't Emma teach her? *She* doesn't have any problems at school, does she?'

'Jim, this isn't a job for a nine-year-old! And anyway, Emma only learned to control *her* power because my mother came and taught her.'

'Marsha, I do *not* want your mother coming here this summer . . . I'm telling you, if I have to listen to one more piece of "motherly" advice, or have you complaining one more time after she's upset you, or sit through yet another story about her freaky garden gnomes . . .'

'Granny's garden gnomes *aren't* freaky,' Saffie muttered without turning round –

which just goes to show that Mum's right when she says that my sister is quite often listening even when you think she's not.

'Listen, Jim, it's true she's not an easy person to have as a house guest, but we need her help, and not *just* because I want Saffie to go to school. We've been lucky until now having wonderful loyal friends living next door, but now we have complete strangers moving in. What if *they* see Saffie in action? I can't handle her on my own any longer, Jim. Yesterday in the supermarket there was this big cardboard advert of a cow beside the dairy counter and Saffie actually made it start mooing. The old lady behind us nearly had a heart attack!'

Saffie was obviously listening to that too, because she started sniggering.

'Look, Saffie!' I gasped, pointing to a large

trampoline that was being carried round the side of our neighbours' house by the two removal men. 'Rosie didn't have one of *those*, did she?'

Saffie pressed her nose against the glass as Mum and Dad came over to see what I was talking about. Just then the man and woman we had spotted earlier came out of their new house and went to unload some stuff from the back of their car. The man pulled out an open cardboard box containing what looked like lots of racks of glass test tubes, and the woman took out a very large and expensive-looking microscope, which she carried into the house as carefully as if it was a newborn baby.

'Don't panic, Marsha,' Dad said, because he knows the way our mother's mind works. 'This doesn't mean they're here to spy on us on behalf of some secret government science department.'

Mum gave a hollow laugh and I could tell that she didn't find his joke funny at all.

No one was talking much as we sat down at the table for dinner that evening. Dad was serving out the shepherd's pie, Mum was dishing out the vegetables and I was helping by fetching everyone a glass of water.

'I don't like broccoli,' Saffie complained in her whiny voice as Mum spooned some on to my sister's plate.

'You ate it at Rosie's house the other day,' our mother said.

'Yes, but Rosie's mum's broccoli tastes nicer than yours!'

'Don't be silly, broccoli is broccoli,' Mum told her firmly.

'Though it *does* depend a bit on how limp you like it,' Dad teased. (When Dad cooks our veggies they're always crisp, whereas Mum likes them a lot softer.)

Just as Mum was giving Dad a glare I noticed that something strange was happening to the broccoli on my little sister's plate. It certainly couldn't be described as limp. The three green stalks on her plate were standing on end and dancing around her blob of mashed potato shouting, '*Please don't eat us, please don't eat us!*'

Mum started to laugh, but Dad didn't. His face went pink and he looked very sternly at my sister. 'Saffie, stop that nonsense at once!'

But Saffie never listens to Dad if she thinks Mum is on her side. And now the veggies on our dad's plate were also rising to the occasion. '*Please, Jim, don't stick that nasty fork into us!'* they shouted as they leaped off his plate on to the table.

It was too much for Dad. Like I said before, our special powers totally freak him out, and he especially hates it when my sister starts messing with his food. He jumped up from the table and shrieked as a piece of dancing broccoli brushed against his finger.

'That's enough, Saffie,' Mum said, struggling to look more serious.

'Yes, Saffie, don't be gross!' I said, because, funny or not, we really aren't supposed to bring food to life, especially not when people are about to eat it. (Though it could have been worse – at least Saffie's dancing veggies didn't have faces.)

Saffie and I were sitting facing the sliding doors that open on to our garden and we both froze as a man suddenly appeared, peering in at us through the glass. I instantly recognized him as our new neighbour – but what was he doing in our back garden?

My sister's broccoli immediately dropped back on to its plate with a splat and our dad's vegetables scattered in every direction all over the tablecloth. And all the time the man from outside was staring in at us.

Our parents turned in their seats to look just as the man waved at us through the window. He was a very large man with dark curly hair and glasses.

'Sorry, chaps! Bell not working!' he mouthed through the glass. He must have come in through the side gate, which Mum is always nagging Dad to keep locked.

As Mum stood up in alarm the man disappeared from view, presumably on his way back round to the front door.

Mum was wearing her most worried frown. 'Do you think he saw anything?'

'Hard to tell,' Dad mumbled. 'He didn't

faint or have a heart attack, so that's a good sign, I guess.'

'I'd better go and see what he wants,' Mum said quickly.

Saffie and I both sat very quietly after that, straining to hear what was happening at the front door. We heard Mum open it and say hello and we heard the front doorbell being rung very loudly twice as Mum clearly took pains to demonstrate that our doorbell *was* in fact working.

I looked across at my sister, who was scowling as she stared very hard out of the window. The hedge between our garden and next door's is very high, but the roof of their shed is just visible over the top. Saffie was staring intensely at that roof.

'Saffie, are you all right?' I asked her softly. She was holding her middle as if she had a tummy ache – which she always does when she's about to use her power to do something difficult.

'I don't like that man,' she declared. 'Rosie's shed doesn't want to live in *his* garden . . .'

'Saffie – NO!' Dad and I burst out at once, but as usual when she has her mind set on something she ignored us.

Outside we could see more of our neighbours' shed appearing as it slowly rose above the hedge. As the bottom of the shed cleared the top of the hedge we saw that Saffie had made it rise up by making it grow two very long spindly legs. But the legs were very wobbly and the shed didn't look as if it was going to be able to stay upright on them for long. Meanwhile the shed's two little square windows had become two round

eyes, the roof was sprouting red curly hair and the door had rotated round to become an oblong mouth. Saffie always likes to give things faces when she brings them to life.

'Saffie, stop it!' I hissed at her, trembling a little.

I'd never attempted to move anything that big myself, chiefly because I was certain I wouldn't be able to. And though I'd known for a while that Saffie's power was stronger than mine, this stunt exceeded even *my* estimation of what she could do.

'Serafina, turn that shed back to normal at once,' Dad ordered her, but he looked terrified and it was plain that he didn't feel the least bit in control of the situation.

'No, Daddy. He'll be *much* happier in

our garden,' Saffie said bossily. 'I shall call him Dennis – that's *long* for Den!' And she giggled as if she thought she was being extremely clever.

'Saffie, you have to do what Dad says,' I told her sharply. I really hate it when it's obvious that *she's* the one in charge instead of Dad.

But she ignored me, her face pink with renewed effort as Dennis the shed lifted up one of his long, skinny legs and placed a great wooden clog of a foot down on our side of the hedge.

'Well done, Dennis!' Saffie exclaimed as he lifted his other leg and began to veer over to our side. 'You've almost done it!'

Dad lost it then. He started threatening Saffie with every completely unrealistic punishment that he could think of, including sitting on the naughty step for the rest of her life and never being allowed out of her bedroom ever again.

Unfortunately that broke her concentration – and this task required all of that.

'Stay focused, Saffie!' I yelled, but it was too late.

The shed instantly lost the life – and the legs – she had just given it.

'Dennis!' Saffie screamed, and all we could hear was a massive crashing and splintering of wood as the shed landed in a heap on our side of the hedge.

CHAPTER 3

When Mum finally finished her conversation with Mr Seaton she came back to join us, by which time there was nothing to see except a pile of wooden debris in our garden. Mum listened with a frown as Dad told her what had happened.

'We did hear a crash but it wasn't obvious where it was coming from,' she said. 'Do you think anyone saw anything?'

'I don't think so.'

Straight away Mum led us outside to inspect the remains of the shed.

Dad shook his head at the mess. 'I suppose I'll have to take all this lot to the dump.'

'Aren't the people next door going to wonder where their shed has gone?' I whispered.

'Of course they'll wonder,' Mum replied, lowering her voice too as she added, 'but I shouldn't think they'll guess the truth, do you?'

'Mummy, Mummy, look!' Saffie was shouting, rushing over to pull something out from under the debris. 'It's Rosie's Supergirl cape!'

She had tugged out the dusty red cape, which was attached to a bright yellow leotard with a silver star on the front. Before anyone could stop her she had rushed off into the house to try them on.

'Rosie always kept her Supergirl costume

hanging up on the back of the den door,' I told my parents. 'It was getting too small for her so she said Saffie could have it when she moved. She must have forgotten to give it to her.'

'Oh, well . . . we'd better check . . . but if that's the case then I'll give it a wash and Saffie can keep it,' Mum said.

Dad looked amused. 'You think it's an appropriate costume for Saffie then?'

'It is *just* a costume, Jim.' Mum lowered her voice to a whisper again. 'It's not going to give her any *extra* powers, is it? Listen, come inside . . . there's something I need to tell you . . .' She started to walk back across our garden to the house, signalling for us to follow her. Once we were safely in the kitchen with the back door shut she turned to my dad. 'Godfrey just told me that his

wife is a scientist . . . a professor in fact . . .
in the field of *human genetics*.'

'You're kidding!' Dad looked aghast.

'I know.' Mum had a very sober look on
her face.

I waited for one of them to explain what
the fuss was about, but they just kept staring
silently at one other.

'So what does that mean?' I asked when
it didn't look as though either of them was
going to tell me.

Mum turned to look at me then. 'Sorry,
Emma. Human genetics is the study of how
we inherit things from our parents.'

'What things?'

Mum sighed. 'Pretty much everything,
darling, though the most obvious traits
that get studied are things like eye colour,
hair colour, height, intelligence and . . .

well . . .' She trailed off.

And suddenly I saw why they were upset.

'Special powers?' I added in a small voice.

Mum nodded and answered hoarsely,
'I'm afraid so. In fact I expect a professor of
human genetics would be *especially* interested
in special powers.'

Dad looked like he felt a bit sick. 'And
what about Godfrey? Don't tell me he's a
scientist too.'

'He works in television.'

'Well,' Dad said, 'at least that's not a
problem.'

But Mum's face remained grim. 'He was
telling me the two of them met while he
was working on a documentary series about
scientific aberrations, human anomalies,
freaks of nature and the like. Apparently
they both share the same passion for

"uncovering the abnormal", as he put it.'

'Oh.' Dad looked sombre.

'Exactly.' She looked at my puzzled face and explained that 'aberration' meant the same as 'anomaly', which basically just meant a difference from the normal.

'Are Saffie and me *anomalies*?' I asked her slowly. 'I mean, *we're* not normal, are we?'

Mum frowned. 'I suppose you *could* describe yourselves as that, although I think it would be more accurate to say that you and Saffie are *exceptional* human beings.'

Dad was nodding his agreement.

'So . . .' Mum continued. 'I think I'd better phone my mother now and ask her to come and help with Saffie as soon as possible. Unless you have any objections, Jim?'

And this time Dad swiftly shook his head.

★

Despite the unease we were all feeling I couldn't help smiling as my little sister came downstairs while Mum was on the phone to Granny. She was dressed in Rosie's Supergirl costume along with some accessories she'd put together herself.

The actual costume consisted of a bright yellow long-sleeved leotard with a silver star on the front and a shiny red cape that buttoned on to the shoulders of the leotard. Saffie had added a pair of stripy tights and her shiny silver wellington boots.

'Hey, Supergirl!' Dad teased, clearly feeling cheerier himself as Saffie twirled around the living room, showing off the big letter 'S' on her cape. 'Haven't you forgotten something?'

'What?' Saffie demanded, stopping in mid-twirl to look down at her costume.

'Superheroes always wear underpants on
the outside of their clothes. I think red ones
would look good. Emma's sure to have a
pair of nice ones you can borrow!'

'Shut up, Dad!' I shrieked, giving him a
shove. 'She is *not* having my pants, OK?'

'Would you three please keep the noise
down . . .' Mum hissed at us, breaking off

her conversation with Granny. 'Saffie, that costume looks lovely on you but it's still very dusty. Before you wear it again it needs to go in the wash!'

'No it doesn't!' Saffie gave Mum a defiant glare before stomping back up the stairs. Sometimes when Saffie finds an outfit that she particularly likes, she insists on wearing it all the time and she'll even go to bed in it rather than let Mum put it in the wash. Mum says it's just a phase she's going through and that she'll grow out of it.

I looked at Dad, who gave me a wink, because we both knew that Mum was going to have a battle on her hands at bedtime that night.

I quickly followed my sister upstairs and knocked on her door before going in. I had decided that I wanted Howard back. I

hadn't really wanted to give him to Saffie in
the first place, but Mum had persuaded me.
She'd said she hoped Howard would have a
steadying influence on Saffie and her dolls.
But since I couldn't see any sign of that, and
Saffie hardly ever bothered to play with him,
I'd decided enough was enough.

Saffie was busy raking through her
underwear drawer, throwing out knickers.
She had obviously taken Dad's comment
seriously.

'All my red pants have got flowers or
fairies on them,' she complained.

'What about these?' I said, picking up a
pair from the floor. But it turned out they
had 'Tuesday' on the front because they came
from her Days of the Week set and, as she
was quick to tell me indignantly, she didn't
just want to be a superhero on Tuesdays!

'I'll see if I've got a plain red pair you can borrow,' I said. 'But, Saffie, please can I have Howard back since you never play with him?'

She nodded, so I went to pick him up from her window ledge before she could change her mind.

I took him straight back to my bedroom, where I sat him down on the bed and decided I really wanted to bring him to life.

So for the second time that day I focused all my concentration on Howard, and was rewarded by having him blink at me before twisting his neck to look around my room.

'Welcome back, Howie. You're going to stay here with me from now on,' I told him fondly as I watched him take in his surroundings.

'Thank goodness,' he said in his deep growly voice, giving me a grateful glance. 'Those dolls were making my head ache with their constant bickering.'

'I'm so sorry I gave you away, Howie,' I added. 'Mum was begging me to do it and eventually I gave in. She knows you're a really sensible bear, you see, and she was hoping you might have a good influence on Saffie.'

Howard bunched together his black stitched eyebrows. 'It will take more than a sensible toy to tame *that* young lady.'

'I know,' I agreed. 'That's why Mum's asking Granny to come and stay with us.'

Howard frowned. 'I'm not sure *that's* such a good idea either. Still . . . I suppose your mother knows what she's doing. Now . . . there's one thing I really must ask of you, Emma . . .' His voice became as gentle as a bear's voice could reasonably be expected to be as he continued, 'My dearest girl, will you please stop calling me *Howie*. I know it's your pet name for me, but I *really* prefer Howard. Howard is a much more *sensible* and grown-up name and I am after all an extremely sensible and grown-up bear.' And he puffed out his chest rather proudly.

I felt my face go a little bit pink as I apologized and assured him that I would try to remember to call him by his proper name from now on.

CHAPTER 4

'Granny! Granny!' Saffie and I exclaimed, rushing down our front path ahead of Mum the following afternoon.

'Come here, my darlings,' Granny cooed, holding out her arms for us to run into them. 'Good grief, Serafina! Whatever are you wearing?'

Saffie was still wearing her new Supergirl outfit, which Mum still hadn't managed to get in the wash, complete with blue underpants over the top because neither of us had been able to find any red ones. She looked just like a character from a comic strip.

Granny was looking exactly the same as usual. She's quite tall and quite plump in the middle, and she has thick dark hair and almond-shaped green eyes, which Dad says are just like a cat's. She also likes to sit in the sun a lot like a cat, which Dad says is the reason her face is quite wrinkly. She doesn't wear a special cape, or a wacky hat, or carry a super-strong handbag to whack villains with as you might expect a supergranny to do. But she did seem to be in possession of a strange new mode of transport.

'Mother, is that vehicle actually *yours*?' Mum asked in amazement as she stared at the small orange van parked in front of our house.

'Do you like it? Much more suitable than my old Mini, don't you think? This way I can take the whole family along when I go anywhere!'

'You don't mean . . .' Mum looked at her quizzically.

'My boys, of course! After all, judging by what you said in your phone call I may be here for some time. I couldn't bear to leave them behind. Besides, one never knows when they might come in useful.' She opened the back of her van for us to look inside.

'Wow!' Saffie exclaimed in delight as we saw that it contained Granny's collection of garden gnomes. There were eleven little statues in total. 'Where's Walter?' Saffie asked when she saw that her favourite gnome was missing.

'Oh, I decided to leave him at home
with your grandpa. Every time I bring that
gnome to life he starts bossing all the other
gnomes about. He has a very strong will of
his own, I'm afraid!'

'Is that because you've brought him
to life too many times, Granny?' I asked,

remembering what she'd taught me about how our powers worked.

Granny nodded. 'I fear that is probably the case, Emma. He was my very first gnome, as you know, and I did rather spoil him.'

Mum was standing listening to all this with her mouth hanging open. 'Mother, I don't think Jim—' she began.

'Leave Jim to me, my dear,' Granny interrupted her swiftly. 'We'll leave the boys here for now and move them later. They're going to have a splendid time in your lovely secluded garden! Now where *is* my favourite son-in-law?'

But Dad had spotted her new van from the window and was already on his way outside to have a closer look. The second he reached Granny he joked, 'I see you've got yourself a new Batmobile! Interesting colour choice!'

And judging by the look Granny gave him I guessed he was probably only her favourite son-in-law because she didn't have any others.

As you've probably realized, unlike Dad my sister and I couldn't be happier when Granny comes to stay. For one thing it's great to have a grown-up around who has the same superpower we do – and who actually encourages us to use it.

As Granny was quick to point out that evening at dinner, *she* believes Saffie and I should learn how to put our special powers to good use in order to help people.

'Like Superman does, you mean?' I asked at once.

'No,' Mum replied firmly before Granny had time to speak. '*Not* like Superman does. Superman has lots of enemies and he's always getting himself into *very* dangerous situations.'

'Besides,' Dad added, winking at me, 'Superman has better powers than you, Emma. I mean you can't *fly*, can you? And you haven't got X-ray vision.'

'Jim . . . please . . .' Granny was giving Dad a very stern look.

'Of course, Superman isn't real,' Dad added hurriedly, 'so he probably isn't a very good example.'

'Who *is* a good example, Granny?' I asked.

But of course Granny couldn't name one, because she doesn't know anyone else in the real world with a superpower.

'You'd think there must be *some* other people like us out there . . .' Mum mused as she stabbed her fork into a squidgy carrot.

'Yes, I mean this can't be the *only* family with an ancestor who was struck by lightning and mutated into a super-being,' Dad added in his teasing voice again.

Granny really doesn't like it when Dad makes fun of our family's special gift. Giving him a cool look, she turned to address Mum. 'Marsha, I am not suggesting the girls dart about like superheroes, helping out complete strangers at huge risk to themselves, but I *do* think—'

'Oh, for goodness sake, whatever's happening now?' Mum broke in impatiently, pointing out into the garden, where it was starting to get dark.

Granny's garden gnomes, who we had already carried into the back garden one by one from the van, were all bending over at the edge of the grass, their shiny bottoms wobbling from side to side as they worked. It looked like they were weeding our flower-bed.

'Mother, you know we have a strict rule about no animations outside the house!' Mum protested. 'What if somebody sees?'

'I do wish you'd stop fretting, Marsha,' Granny retorted. 'Your hedges are far too high for anyone to see into the garden . . . You're lucky . . . When *I* tried to screen off *my* little garden, I got a letter from the council telling me I'd overdone it and that my neighbours had complained. You'd think they'd be grateful to have a bit of privacy themselves instead of making all that fuss about the lack of light, wouldn't you?'

Saffie had gone over to the patio doors to watch the gnomes at work. She was clearly fascinated by seeing so many of them all in motion at the same time. (The most I can do is two toys at once, though I know Saffie can manage three.) Granny says that *multi-animating* is just like being the conductor of an orchestra. First you set one instrument off and then another, keeping each one in mind while managing the orchestra as a whole.

'Look!' Saffie suddenly exclaimed, pointing to the hedge between our garden and the next. A couple of seconds later a blond head appeared over the top – then disappeared just as quickly. 'Emma, it's that boy!' Saffie shrieked. 'He must be on his trampoline.'

'What boy?' Mum asked now.

'Yes, what boy?' Dad echoed.

I hadn't yet told our parents about the encounter we'd had with the boy next door, so I quickly filled them in. At the same time Granny started de-animating her garden gnomes one by one at top speed. Mum was looking stunned as if she was only just realizing the full implications of our new neighbours owning a trampoline.

'Listen, let's not get too paranoid, shall

we?' Dad said. 'This trampoline is probably just a perfectly innocent toy . . .'

'A toy that doubles as a spying device, more likely!' Mum muttered.

'Don't worry, it won't be operational for much longer in any case,' Granny said grimly. 'I've disabled plenty of spying devices in my time and this one shouldn't be too difficult!'

Dad was smiling now. 'Don't tell me, Supergran! You and your gnomes are going over there tonight to rip it to bits with your gardening forks?'

Granny looked across at him with an ultra-straight face. 'Make fun of me if you like, Jim, if it helps you deal with this . . . but Marsha is right. These new neighbours of yours are a serious threat and we can't just ignore them.' She turned back to Mum. 'Tomorrow I shall take Saffie under my wing. We'll soon have her more in control of her power. Emma, you can help too. I gather you don't use your gift very much these days, so it will do you good to have a bit of practice.'

I flushed because it's true that I don't use my superpower nearly as much as I used to – at least not in front of my family. Ever since I realized that my gift isn't as strong as Saffie's I've tended to use it just when I'm on my own.

Granny looked at my sister, who still had her face pressed against the window looking out at the boy. Granny cleared her throat loudly as if she was about to make an important announcement. '*Be selective. Be accurate. Be discreet.* Those are the golden rules one needs to live by if one is born with a special power, Serafina.'

Unfortunately it seemed that Saffie truly wasn't listening this time, because she said, 'Mum, shall I make the trampoline come to life right now and tip him off?'

'Of course not!' Mum replied crossly, rushing to pull her away from the window.

'*Discreet*?' Dad responded to Granny's words of advice with a chuckle. 'Is *that* what you call a bright orange van full of garden gnomes?'

Granny glared at him. 'A van has no windows at the back, therefore it is *very* discreet, thank you, Jim. Now . . . if you don't mind I'd like to finish my dinner . . . And, Marsha, *please* tell me you're not allowing my granddaughters to leave all that food on their plates. Though I must say these greens might be a bit more appetizing if they weren't *quite* so well cooked . . .'

CHAPTER 5

'Granny, are you going to start teaching
Saffie today?' I asked as I passed her the
cornflakes at breakfast the next morning.
Saffie was upstairs getting dressed. Judging
by the time she was taking I was guessing
she'd got sidetracked into playing with
her dolls again, but as it was the summer
holidays and there was no school Mum said
it didn't really matter.

Mum was unloading the washing machine
and Dad had just left for work.

Granny nodded. 'I certainly am,

Emma – and you can help me. I think a game of frisbee with my garden gnomes will start us off nicely.' Before Mum could protest Granny said, 'Don't worry, Marsha, I saw your neighbours leave in their car just now. They won't see anything. Which reminds me . . . I must do something about that boy's wretched trampoline today . . .' She frowned. 'Marsha, just look at all that washing! I really can't understand why you don't get the girls to help you more.'

'They do help me, Mother. They often peg it out on the line.'

'You know very well what I mean,' Granny said impatiently. 'There's really no need to spend all the time you do on all these household chores.'

'Mother, Jim would freak out if the

housework started doing itself. He's not like Dad, you know. He won't just withdraw into his own little world and pretend it's not happening.'

Granny gave her a narrow-eyed look. 'I wouldn't say your father *withdraws*, Marsha. And regarding the housework, I gave him the option years ago of doing it all himself if he didn't approve of my methods.'

'I know – I remember you gave me the same generous option when I was a teenager,' Mum said, before promptly disappearing outside with the washing basket.

Granny was frowning after Mum as she murmured, 'Come on, Emma . . . let's go and find your sister . . .'

★

'What we need to work on first, Saffie, is improving your concentration,' Granny was saying half an hour later as she dug out our frisbee from our under-the-stairs cupboard. Mum had gone to the shops, making us promise to listen carefully for any sign of our neighbours returning. 'That's the first thing I worked on with *you* when you were little, isn't it, Emma?' Granny added, throwing the frisbee to me to catch, which we are absolutely not allowed to do inside the house.

I nodded. Granny's lessons had pretty much all been about concentration as far as I recalled. 'We played lots of memory games,' I said. 'It was fun. You know, Saffie, like when we're in the car and we play In My Picnic Basket I Packed . . . and you have to remember everything that's in it.'

68

'I don't like that game,' Saffie said. 'I like pretend games better – or playing outside.'

'Which is why I want to make use of the garden while your neighbours are out,' Granny said promptly. 'You have to learn how to stay more focused when you are using your power, Saffie. If you get interrupted in the middle of an animation you have to practise keeping *some* of your attention on your chosen object, even if you are also forced to focus elsewhere. Otherwise incidents like the one with your shed yesterday will keep on happening. Do you understand?'

'That wasn't *my* fault . . .' Saffie whined, glowering defensively at the mention of Dennis.

Granny laughed. 'It never is, my darling . . . Now listen to me . . . you and Emma have both been born with an incredible gift . . . but you need to learn how to use it responsibly . . .'

'That means sensibly and safely, Saffie,' I told her in my most grown-up big-sister voice.

Saffie was still frowning, but I could tell we had her attention.

'We will now have a game of frisbee in the garden,' Granny continued. 'It will be a perfectly normal game but with one exception. Saffie, you must choose one of my gnomes to bring to life so that he can join in the game. Then I want you to play frisbee with us while also keeping the gnome animated. It will be excellent practice in how to split your attention effectively!'

So we went out into the back garden and

Saffie immediately concentrated on making Granny's second-oldest gnome, Cedric, spring into action. Cedric is a very friendly-looking garden gnome with bright blue eyes, white hair and a long white beard. He wears green dungarees over a white shirt with the sleeves rolled up, a pair of black boots and an orange pointy hat. He also carries a fishing rod with a grey plastic fish dangling from the end.

As soon as Cedric came to life he tightened his grip on his rod and started to panic about where to put his fish – which had also come to life and was flapping about furiously on the end of his fishing line.

Granny was flapping too. When she's in her own garden she always drops Cedric's fish straight into the garden pond – but unfortunately we don't have one. She

turned to me. 'Emma, would you go and fill the washing-up bowl with cold water, please, and bring it out here as quickly as you can.'

By the time I got back outside, everyone was looking super-stressed.

'Over here, quickly!' yelled Cedric. He plopped the now weakly flapping fish into the bowl and let out a relieved sigh as it revived and began to swim around. (Only when *he* became an ordinary garden gnome again would his fish turn back to plastic.)

'Cedric, do you know how to play frisbee?' Saffie asked him after we had spent a few minutes watching the fish.

'Of course I know how to play frisbee! Frisbee, rounders, piggy in the middle, hide-and-seek, ring-a-ring o' roses . . . you name it, I can play it!' Cedric boasted.

'OK then! Let's start!' Saffie sang out, running into the middle of the grass with the frisbee and shouting, 'Here, Emma!' as she hurled it at me.

'Great throw, Saffie!' Cedric praised her, and when I caught it he jumped up and down and clapped.

Cedric proved to be a fantastic player himself, leaping into the air to catch the plastic disc without fail each time as Saffie giggled in delight.

Granny was clearly as impressed by Cedric's – and Saffie's – performance as I was. She surveyed my sister who, as well as keeping Cedric on top form, was also managing to throw and catch the frisbee herself when required. 'Saffie, you are much more talented than I realized,' she told her.

'That must be why *I'm* so talented,' Cedric declared. 'After all, talent begets talent, does it not?'

'Cedric, stop boasting and CATCH!' I yelled.

And that was when it all went wrong.

Just as Cedric leaped up to catch the frisbee I had hurled, my little sister noticed her Supergirl costume hanging out on the washing-line to dry. Mum must have decided to put it in the wash after all without telling her.

'Hey! I wanted to wear that today! I was looking for it everywhere!' Saffie exclaimed, forgetting Cedric in an instant. As she stomped over to the washing-line, the gnome fell with a thud to the ground, no longer animated, and the frisbee sailed on over the hedge into our neighbours' garden.

'Serafina!' Granny shouted crossly as she rushed over to check on Cedric. 'This is just what you are *not* to do! Poor Cedric is going to have a very sore head when he next comes to life – I just hope he doesn't have concussion.'

'I don't think you can get concussion when you don't have a brain,' I said, thinking back to Dad's reaction the last time Mum had been in a panic after her precious Elvira had fallen off Saffie's window ledge and banged her head.

But Saffie hadn't finished venting her anger yet. She was standing staring up at her bedroom window with a flushed face and a certain glint in her eyes that spelled trouble.

'How do you *know* a garden gnome doesn't have a brain?' shouted a familiar voice from above our heads, and Granny and I looked up to see Dorothy the rag doll standing on Saffie's window ledge, pressing her nose against the glass to look down at us. Elvira was standing beside her. The small window above them was open so we could hear them easily.

'If he *does* have a brain then it's probably in his bottom,' Elvira joked, 'just like yours, Dorothy!'

'Elvira, you may be the longest serving doll in this family, but you've gone too far this time,' Dorothy snapped, and she gave the other doll a very angry shove.

Elvira screamed as she toppled backwards off the window ledge and disappeared from view.

Granny was gazing at my sister thoughtfully. 'That child is all over the place! I can see why your mother needs me to take her in hand.' She put on her sternest voice as she called out, 'Serafina, please come here right now.'

Saffie ignored her. Like I said before,

Saffie hates being bossed around.

'Young lady, this is no way to behave!' Granny called across sternly to my sister. 'Your mother thinks it's just your attention span that's the problem, but I'm not so sure! If you can't control those dolls of yours then perhaps we should take them away.'

Saffie immediately stopped laughing and looked angry again. 'NO!' she shouted stubbornly, stamping her foot and running headlong into the house before Granny could stop her.

'Serafina, come back here!' Granny shouted, but she got no response.

'I think she's cross all the time because she doesn't understand what's happening to her,' I murmured. I was remembering what it was like to be my sister's age and having to deal with a so-called 'gift' that would freak out most grown-ups.

'Neither did *I* understand it when I was her age, but I still behaved myself,' Granny snapped.

I felt myself becoming more and more protective of my little sister as Granny ranted on about how Saffie wasn't so much confused as just plain naughty. 'That child's a time bomb waiting to go off!' Granny finally concluded. 'I can see now why your poor mother is so worried! I had no idea Serafina had turned into such a handful!'

For the first time ever I actually shouted at Granny. 'Stop saying horrible things about Saffie! It's not *her* fault that one of *your* stupid ancestors was struck by lightning and got genetically mutated into a super-being, is it?'

Granny let out a gasp, then a snort of laughter, before rounding on me. 'Young lady, in case you've forgotten how these things work – that stupid person was *your* ancestor too!'

Just then we heard a creaking sound coming from the other side of the hedge. Someone was jumping up and down on the trampoline next door.

Granny and I stood still, staring at each other. Whoever it was would have heard everything. 'Let's go inside now,' Granny said, looking pale.

But Saffie must have gone straight upstairs to her bedroom, because the main window was now wide open and she was leaning out of it holding Elvira, who she must have rescued from the bedroom floor.

'Cedric wants to play frisbee again!' a

very wild and worked-up Saffie shouted
down at us.

Cedric sprang back to life and let out a
groan as he felt the pain in his head. Then
he started to fuss about the whereabouts
of his fishing rod (which was on the
grass beside him) and his fish (which had
remained in the washing-up bowl). At the
same time Dorothy, who was still on Saffie's
window ledge, screamed as Elvira's foot
dealt her a well-aimed kick that sent her
flying right out of the open window.

At that exact moment a head appeared
for a few seconds on the other side of our
neighbours' hedge. I'd expected to see the
boy from next door, but instead it was
his dad – Godfrey Seaton – who was on
the trampoline. As he jumped higher and
higher, getting a better view of our garden

with each bounce, his breathless voice called out to us, 'Don't mind me! Just taking a spot of exercise!' And all the time his inquisitive eyes were taking in everything.

It was then that Cedric picked up his fishing rod and announced that he was going to catch his fish, even if he did have to make do with a washing-up bowl instead of a proper garden pond.

And Godfrey Seaton let out a shriek like the kind you might make on a very fast and scary fairground ride. It was half terrified and half excited.

CHAPTER 6

When Mum got back from the shops a little later and heard what we had to say she just stared at the three of us in horror.

'So you're saying he saw Cedric coming to life *and* he saw Dorothy already animated as she fell out of the window *and* he overheard Emma yelling out that we were a family of mutant super-beings,' Mum summarized, glaring at all three of us but particularly at Granny.

I gulped. 'Sorry, Mum.' It sounded even worse, put like that.

'I did check that their car was still gone before we went outside,' Granny defended herself, looking flushed. 'I don't know why I didn't hear them coming back. Normally my hearing is very good.'

'Superman would have heard them,' Saffie piped up, looking thoughtful, 'because *he* has superhuman hearing.' Saffie wasn't poking fun at Granny. She was quite serious, having recently started to take a great interest in all fictional superheroes.

'The trouble is, we were making too much noise ourselves,' I put in quickly before Granny could take offence at the Superman reference.

But Granny wasn't really listening to my sister. 'Quite frankly, Marsha, I don't know what planet you're on in any case if you think that your *last* neighbours didn't notice anything!' she told Mum, having clearly had enough of being glared at accusingly. 'From what I hear, Saffie played there unsupervised all the time – and don't tell me Rosie never got to see her in action!'

'Rosie's family were our friends, Mother,' Mum said hotly. 'Yes, they found out that we weren't a normal family, but they also knew how important it was to keep that a secret. Whereas with these new neighbours things are quite different.'

'Our new neighbours are *very* dangerous,' Saffie suddenly said. 'If they find out what Emma and me can do they might take us away to a science laboratory and do experiments on us. That's why Emma and me have to stay away from them.'

Granny looked horrified. 'Really, Marsha, was it really necessary to—'

'Yes, Mother, it was,' Mum told her sharply, before turning and ushering Saffie in front of her out of the room.

After they had gone I turned to Granny, but she spoke before I could. 'I'm afraid my visit hasn't gone very well so far, Emma. I think it might be better if I leave tomorrow.'

'Oh, no, Granny, please don't go . . .' I begged her.

'I think I must. Though there is one other thing I intend to do before I leave . . .'

'*What* thing?' I asked, hearing distant alarm bells starting to ring.

'I shall keep my promise about deactivating that wretched trampoline!'

I decided to go round to our neighbours' garden later that afternoon to collect our frisbee. I could have asked Granny to get it back for us, but somehow I didn't like the idea of Granny making our frisbee grow legs and scuttle back to us over the lawn. Besides, I wanted to rescue the teddy bear Saffie had binned before it was too late. I didn't tell anyone where I was going. Mum was having a lie-down upstairs and Saffie was playing with her dolls in her bedroom. Granny had gone out for a walk after lunch and hadn't come back yet, so I reckoned the coast was clear.

It's easy to get into the back garden of Rosie's old house because there's no side gate. Our new neighbours' car was in the drive, but there didn't seem to be anybody about.

At the near end of the garden everything looked the same as usual – the large neat-looking lawn, the leafy bushes on either side of it that are great for playing hide-and-seek, and the two huge trees which Dad is always saying ought to be cropped. It was the far end of the garden that looked different. I could see the trampoline at the bottom of the garden next to the hedge, and where the shed had been there was a bit of debris and a rectangle of mud.

Suddenly I heard the back door opening and the sound of voices. Straight away I ran to the nearest bush, knowing it was the best one to hide inside.

'It's polite to ask before you enter someone else's property,' hissed the bush as I parted its leaves.

I nearly jumped out of my skin – and for the first time I realized how Dad must feel when his shoes suddenly start talking to him.

I instantly turned round to look for my sister. It must be Saffie who was making the bush talk, but there was no sign of her.

'Come on in before they see you,' hissed the bush again, and that's when I realized that the voice wasn't coming from the bush itself.

'I'm sorry,' I stammered as I recognized the boy who was already sitting on the ground inside the central hollow. 'I was just coming to get my frisbee and—'

'It's OK,' the boy whispered. 'But hurry up and come inside. My mum and dad are going to see you in a minute if you don't and then my hiding place will be ruined.'

I quickly scrambled to the middle and sat down cross-legged on the ground, flushing bright red as my knee bumped against his.

We waited in silence while his parents

walked past. They seemed to be arguing about how unlikely it was that a garden shed could just disappear into thin air.

'So what's your name?' the boy asked me when they were out of earshot.

'Emmeline,' I replied. 'But I don't like being called that. Everyone calls me Emma.'

He grinned. 'Ditto,' he said.

'Ditto?'

'Ditto, I hate my stupid name. It's Sigmund, but everyone calls me Ziggy.'

'Oh.' I couldn't help liking him a tiny bit suddenly.

Then he said, 'Great puppet show on your kid sister's window ledge the other morning.'

I frowned, thinking back to what he had said that morning. 'You didn't seem to like it at the time.'

He pulled an apologetic face. 'Sorry if I wasn't very nice. I was in a bad mood because I really didn't want to move here.'

'Why not?' I asked. 'Don't you like Rosie's house?' Too late I realized how daft that sounded.

'Oh, it's not the new house so much

as the new neighbours,' he joked, giving me a teasing grin. 'No, seriously . . . We moved partly because Mum's got a job at the university here and she doesn't want to commute and partly because Dad . . .' He broke off. 'Well, it's a bit complicated, actually.' He barely paused for breath before continuing, 'So what's all this about your family being some kind of super-mutants? My dad says he reckons you can control stuff with your minds or something like that. He even reckons you levitated our garden shed! Can you believe that?'

I immediately went cold inside. I did my best to fake a light-hearted laugh but it didn't really come out right. I felt as if I was going to throw up.

Ziggy was staring at me intently. 'What's

wrong? I thought you'd say my dad must be mad.'

In the last few years I've had to tell my fair share of lies in order to protect our family, but for some reason I found this lie really difficult. 'Of course he must be mad,' I murmured. 'He sounds completely crazy.'

'That's what *I* said,' Ziggy continued, still looking at me quite closely, 'and so did Mum at first. But then Dad overheard something when he was on the trampoline this morning, something that got Mum excited too. It was something about genetic mutations turning people into super-beings. I told them they were *both* mad then, but Dad kept going on about how the weirdest things can sometimes turn out to be just on your doorstep.'

I swallowed. 'So what would your mum

do if she found someone with a . . . well . . . a special power, for instance?'

'Oh, she'd want to study them forever, I guess, and run lots and lots of tests on them.' He laughed. 'A bit like she does with the mutant rats she keeps in her laboratory.'

I was trying really hard to keep my voice from trembling as I asked, 'And what about your dad? Why is he so interested in us?'

'Oh, Dad just gets a real buzz from tracking down really weird people and exposing them . . . sorry . . . *interviewing* them on his TV show. His programme is called *Freaky Families on the Sofa.* You've probably never seen it because it's on late at night on a satellite channel, but he reckons Channel 4 would take it if he could find one really brilliant family.'

'What sort of family?' I croaked.

'Well, a really long time ago he worked on a documentary series about aliens. Mum got really excited about that because she believes a lot of stuff that most other scientists don't – that aliens and UFOs really do exist, for example. I know he'd love to do a programme about a family of aliens. Then Mum could investigate them from a scientific stance and she'd probably even get to appear on his programme. So would the aliens of course.'

'Well *we're* not aliens, in case that's what you're thinking!' I snapped defensively, then ran my tongue over my extremely dry lips and muttered, 'Anyway, aliens don't exist. Your mum sounds just as mad as your dad.' I scrambled out from under the bush, not caring if Ziggy's parents saw me. I was so upset that I forgot all about collecting our frisbee as I tore off in the direction of home.

And I also forgot about rescuing Ziggy's teddy bear, even though I passed right by the bins and the following day was bin day.

CHAPTER 7

I told Mum everything as soon as I got in.

For a minute or two she seemed too shocked to speak. She just sat down and hid her face in her hands.

'We could always move house ourselves,' I suggested when her silence started to scare me.

'No,' she said, looking up sharply. 'I like our house and I don't see why we should let some nosy neighbour run us out of it. Besides, if you start running away all the time then it never stops.' Mum had hated having to move home all the time while she was growing up, I remembered now. My mother's whole demeanour was changing as she spoke, as if she had suddenly decided that giving up wasn't an option.

'First we need to explain away what our neighbours have already seen, which means that basically we have to think up a really good cover story,' she told me. 'That shouldn't be too difficult since most people are desperate to be offered a sensible explanation after they've seen such weird goings-on. The second part is going to be harder. We *have* to find a way of motivating Saffie to be more cautious. The trouble is she's too young to really understand the full extent of what could happen if the truth came out.' She sighed. 'At least we don't have to worry about the trampoline for much longer. Your grandmother is going to deal with that.'

'What will Granny *do* to it?' I asked curiously.

Mum smiled ever so slightly. 'Just wait and see.'

'But, Mum,' I reminded her, thinking about the look on our new neighbour's face as he had bounced up and down while taking in everything in our garden. 'Ziggy's dad actually *saw* Cedric come to life!'

'I'm afraid that's going to be very tricky to explain away,' Mum agreed. She was about to continue when we heard a commotion that sounded like it was coming from Saffie's room.

'It's those dolls again,' Mum said, frowning. 'You know, I really don't like the way Elvira and Dorothy are turning out.

Saffie is having a very bad influence on both of them, I'm afraid, and Dorothy had a very cheeky personality in the first place, which doesn't help.'

'Do you want me to go upstairs and speak to them?' I asked.

'No, thank you, Emma.' Mum looked more determined than I had seen her in a long while. 'I think I'll go and sort out those dolls myself. And while I'm up there I'll have a go at sorting out your little sister as well. I think it's time I started to threaten her with the kind of consequences she *does* understand.'

And with that Mum left the room.

By the time Dad got home Saffie was in bed having cried – or more accurately tantrummed – herself to sleep. Mum had confiscated Elvira and Dorothy and told my sister that she could only have them back when she was prepared to make them come to life in a more responsible manner.

'Jim, could you help Mother put her gnomes back in the van straight away?' Mum asked after she had related everything that had taken place. 'I'm afraid they might prove too much of a temptation for Saffie if they're left where she can see them out in the garden.'

'A temptation for Saffie? What about for your mother?' Dad joked just as Granny came into the room with a tray of drinks for all of us. Avoiding her scowl he quickly went on, 'Anyway, isn't it a bit late to hide the fact that our gnomes can come to life when Godfrey has already seen Cedric in action?'

'And we still have to explain away
what Saffie did to their shed,' I reminded
everybody.

'Maybe we should think about the shed
issue first,' Mum said.

Mum and Granny looked at each other,
both of them frowning, as if they were now
consulting a joint mental database of suitable
excuses.

'It was vandals!' Mum declared almost at
once. 'Some very strong and high-spirited
vandals who thought it would be funny to
toss the remains of the shed into *our* garden
after they'd knocked it down.'

Granny immediately nodded her approval.
'*Vandals* can be used to explain away a large
variety of different things, Emma,' she told
me. 'In fact the letter "V" should always
come to mind whenever a problem arises.

V for Vandals, V for Ventriloquism, V for Vivid imagination. These are three of your first-line excuses and you'll remember them if you remember the letter "V".'

'But what about the stuff Ziggy's dad overheard *me* saying?' I asked them, not seeing how they could possibly explain away everything. 'About how our ancestor got mutated into a super-being by a stroke of lightning?'

Before Mum and Granny could answer, Dad jumped straight in. 'You've got a very *vivid* imagination, Emma. And you've been watching too many Superman films.'

Mum smiled and Granny nodded approvingly.

'Very good, Jim,' Granny said. 'I can see you're starting to think like one of us at last. Now . . . let's think about how to tackle our most difficult problem – the fact that that hideous man actually *saw* Cedric come to life.'

'I've got an idea about that,' I said shyly. 'But it's quite risky . . . You see, it involves Cedric again.'

CHAPTER 8

The next morning my mother took me with her to go and call on our new neighbours. It was to be my job to put my plan into action when the time came. For now, Cedric was standing on the doorstep next to us while we waited for someone to answer the bell.

'Good morning,' Mum said as Ziggy's mother opened the door.

Professor Seaton was a tall thin woman with straight dark blonde hair like Ziggy's, and she looked extremely surprised to see us.

'I do hope you don't mind us calling

round uninvited like this,' Mum gushed, 'but we wanted to welcome you to the street and Emma thought your son might like to see her new remote-controlled gnome.'

At that point I fought back a fit of the giggles as Professor Seaton invited us in.

Mum carried Cedric inside, still in his statue form, and left him standing just inside the door. Ziggy's mum was calling out for her husband to join us with what sounded like a note of panic in her voice.

'What is it, Iris? You know I'm on my way to observe our neighbours!' Mr Seaton grumbled from upstairs.

'Our neighbours are *here*, dear!' his wife called out, giving Mum and me a self-conscious smile.

'Oh.' Ziggy's dad arrived downstairs

dressed in a jumper and baggy jogging bottoms with a pair of binoculars in his hand. He flushed bright red when he saw us. 'Why on earth didn't you say who it was, my dear? Shouldn't we be getting them a cup of tea or something . . .'

'Do you *drink* tea?' Ziggy's mother asked us, her tone of voice implying that she thought we might only be able to ingest some other kind of drink from our own planet.

Mum nodded, smiling, 'But please don't worry about that now. We won't stay long. Is your son in? Emma wanted to show him Cedric.'

'Cedric?' Mr Seaton asked.

'Her remote-controlled gnome.' Mum pointed back to the front door where Cedric was standing. 'Show them how he works, Emma.'

Trying to stop my hand from trembling, I took the remote-control box we'd borrowed from Saffie's toy robot out of my jacket pocket. Now I had to do two things at once. I had to bring Cedric to life while pretending to operate the remote control. Cedric and I had practised what was to happen next over and over, but I was still terrified something would go wrong.

Cedric had been given strict instructions to remain still to start with, even after he had been brought to life. When I started pressing buttons on the remote control and telling everyone what I was doing, then he was to move in a slightly jerky manner in accordance with what I said.

So as I said, 'He can walk forwards when I press this button,' he was meant to walk briskly towards me.

I inwardly breathed a sigh of relief as Cedric walked robot-like across the carpet.

'He can speak too,' I said, making a big thing of pressing a different button.

'Where – is – the – gar – den – pond?' Cedric said in a stilted voice. He was still walking and, as Godfrey stepped aside, Cedric marched past him and through the open door into the lounge.

Ziggy's mum was smiling. 'See, Godfrey! I told you there must be a simple explanation,' she said.

But Mr Seaton was shaking his head. 'That is not the gnome that I saw. The one I saw was walking and talking quite naturally – not at all like this little robot.'

At that Cedric twirled round, clearly furious. 'Robot? Who are you calling a robot?' he shouted.

The Seatons instantly froze with their mouths hanging open, and Mum looked at me with panic in her eyes. Cedric was standing absolutely still again, but his face looked cross.

I felt a bit sick because I couldn't think how we were ever going to explain our way out of this one.

Suddenly I thought of the toy hamster Saffie had been given for Christmas – you turned it on by pressing its paw and then it repeated back everything you said to it in its own funny squeaky voice.

'You can press a button that makes him repeat back the last word you say to him,' I explained. 'And . . . and he can do even more than that. It's really clever! If I say, "You're a garden *gnome*," he'll say, "*Gnome? Who are you calling a gnome*?" Or if I say,

"You're being an *idiot*!" he'll say, "*Idiot?* Who are you calling an *idiot*?" Or I can say, "You little *monkey*!" and he'll say, "*Monkey?* Who are you calling a *monkey*?" Or if I say—'

'Thank you, Emma, I think we get the idea,' Mum said swiftly, though I could tell she was impressed by my ingenuity. 'Why don't you make him dance for us now?'

So I pointed the remote control at Cedric again and he obligingly began to twirl about

in a not too robotic way, humming to himself at the same time.

'Amazing,' Ziggy's mother said. 'From a distance anyone would think it was a real little gnome-man.' She looked at her husband sharply. 'And you *did* see it from a distance, Godfrey . . . for a few seconds, in fact, while bouncing up and down on a trampoline . . .'

Godfrey was nodding his agreement, clearly doubting himself now that our much more likely explanation was being given the seal of approval by his wife.

I realized that they were both looking quite relieved. It seemed that even a professor who was interested in aliens and a TV presenter who needed an alien family for his TV show would *still* rather discover that their next-door neighbours were boring old humans after all.

'Well, we'll leave you in peace,' Mum said, giving me a look that told me it was time to turn Cedric back into a normal garden gnome again.

'Where's Ziggy?' I asked as his mother showed us to the door.

'Oh, he's upstairs looking for his favourite teddy that got lost in the move.' His mother sighed. 'He's never been much of a one for cuddly toys, but he's had this particular teddy since he was a baby . . .'

I gasped, because of course I had completely forgotten about rescuing Ziggy's bear from the dustbin.

As she spoke she opened the front door for us and we saw the big lorry that collects all the rubbish driving away from us down the street.

'Oh no!' I felt terrible.

'What's wrong?' Ziggy's mum asked me, but of course I couldn't tell her.

I'm not sure what I'd have done if I'd been left to deal with the situation on my own. But straight away I saw Saffie standing alone on the pavement outside our house. She had her back to us and she was looking in the direction of the dustbin lorry. And she was clutching her tummy.

'Oh no,' Mum murmured just as Ziggy came thundering down the stairs looking really upset.

'Mum, I've looked and looked and I can't find Henry anywhere!' he exclaimed, rubbing his eyes as if he had been crying. Then he saw that we were there and he suddenly looked very stiff and awkward.

Before anyone could speak, the rubbish

lorry screeched to a dramatic halt and a voice that sounded like it was coming from a megaphone boomed out, 'STAND BACK, CITIZENS! I DO BELIEVE I AM GOING TO BE SICK!'

'What the . . . ?' Even Mum looked astounded.

The rear of the lorry had turned into a rectangular face with knitted eyebrows and big square eyes. The opening for the rubbish bags had become a huge gaping mouth that let out a loud belch followed by a terrible retching sound. Then the lorry began to spew out its load, ejecting bag after bag of stinking rubbish on to the street.

The driver had already jumped down from his cab to see what was going on, and the other bin men were standing staring in disbelief at the rubbish that was piling up

behind their vehicle. People were starting to come out of their houses to see what was happening, and cars were screeching to a halt in the street.

I could tell that Mum was quickly putting two and two together, though she obviously didn't know *why* my sister was doing this. I reckoned I did. Saffie must have seen the bins being collected and remembered about Ziggy's bear. My little sister often felt sorry after she'd done something naughty and wanted to put it right, but usually by that time it was too late.

Mum was saying a hurried goodbye to Ziggy's mum, who fortunately was too short-sighted without her glasses to see exactly what was happening at the other end of the street. I rushed to join Saffie, desperate to get to her before Mum.

Thankfully she had stopped animating the lorry and nobody else seemed to have noticed the face except Mum – and possibly Ziggy's dad, judging by the way he had just rushed off to find his video camera.

'Saffie, what are you doing?' I hissed.

'I was telling Granny how much I miss Elvira and Dorothy since Mummy took them away from me,' Saffie said in a small voice. 'And it made me think about that boy and how he must be missing his teddy bear. And I was going to fetch it back for him when I saw the bin lorry taking away all the rubbish.'

'There's no way the bin men will let us search through all those bags to find Ziggy's bear,' I said, trying to think what to do.

'Maybe I can make Ziggy's bear come

to *us*?' Saffie said. 'But we have to get closer.'

'OK, then.' I held her hand. 'Come on.'

We pretended not to hear Mum calling after us as we ran down the street, heading for the stranded truck and the heap of spewed-out black bags. Many of the refuse sacks were torn or split open but there was no sign of Ziggy's bear among the loose rubbish lying around.

'Do you remember him clearly enough to picture him in your mind?' I asked Saffie urgently.

She nodded and stood still on the pavement, closing her eyes. As Saffie did her best to bring the bear to life with her special power, I scoured the rubbish sacks looking for any sign of movement.

Ziggy arrived, out of breath from running.

'What are you two doing? Your mum says you've got to come back at once.'

'Shush!' I put my finger to my lips, pointing at Saffie.

'Look, what's that?' someone shouted.

A lot of the bags had fallen together in a massive heap to form a black mountain of rubbish sacks. And now something small and brown and furry was dragging itself up to the top of that mountain, paw by shuddering paw. As he reached the top, the little creature stood up and knocked a greasy crisp packet off his head.

'It's a rat! Stand back, everyone! It's a rat!' shouted one of our neighbours.

This gave the bear such a fright it lost its footing and started to tumble down the bin-bag mountain as several people backed away very rapidly.

I quickly rushed forward, ignoring everyone's cries for me to come back. I reached the pile of rubbish sacks and grabbed the bear. 'You're safe now, Henry,' I whispered as the frightened toy let out a relieved sob. 'I'll take you back to Ziggy.'

'Oh, thank you!' The bear gave me the friendliest of growls before Saffie withdrew her power and he became a normal toy again.

Ziggy looked shocked and stood gaping at me, his arms remaining firmly at his sides, as I held Henry out for him to take.

When our mothers arrived, looking a mixture of stern and relieved, and Ziggy's dad appeared, extremely overexcited and armed with a massive camera, Ziggy slowly held out his hand to take his toy bear.

'Are you OK?' I asked him softly.

He nodded. 'Thanks,' he mumbled.

'You're welcome,' Saffie chirped up, as if to remind us that *she* should be the one he was thanking, not me. She had clearly forgotten that she was the one who had put Henry in harm's way in the first place.

'Thanks, Saffie,' Ziggy said at once.

'Yes, well done, Saffie,' I said, giving her a hug. I knew that she had put us in a lot of danger by using her power in full view of all our neighbours like that, but I couldn't start telling her off. After all, I hadn't exactly discouraged her.

CHAPTER 9

'Of course, I was only *so* bothered about losing Henry because I knew Mum would be upset,' Ziggy said, doing his best to sound cool as we sat chatting in his back garden. Saffie had gone straight home with Mum, whereas I had decided to pop next door first to collect our frisbee.

'Sure,' I said with a disbelieving grin.

He smiled, then lowered his voice as he said, 'Listen, I'm really sorry about my dad shoving his stupid camera in your faces like that. I think he just got really excited because he saw Saffie make that lorry come to life the same as I did and, well . . . families who might be aliens just aren't that easy to find.'

. 'I keep telling you – we're *not* aliens,' I said sharply.

'I know, I know . . . I'm just saying he was excited because he *thought* all over again that you could be, that's all . . .'

I took a deep breath and did my best to calm down. After all, Ziggy had been brilliant at handling his dad for us just now. His dad had taken so long rushing around the house trying to find his camera that, by the time he got back outside, the lorry had lost its lifelike features. As everybody else was talking about how there had to be a fault in the garbage-disposal mechanism inside the lorry, Mr Seaton gradually came round to the idea that they must be right and that he had imagined the face. As for the lorry's voice, Ziggy had helped us there as well.

'I thought it was really funny when one of the bin men pretended to be the lorry shouting out that it was going to be sick, didn't you, Dad?' he had said. And his dad had agreed, clearly not wanting to admit that he had thought the voice had come from the lorry itself.

I looked at Ziggy gratefully as I remembered how well he had covered for us. But at the same time it didn't really make any sense to me why he would.

'Ziggy, why are you taking *my* family's side in this?' I asked him. 'I mean, why are you helping *us* instead of your own dad?'

Ziggy frowned, plucking at the grass

while he clearly tried to decide whether or not to tell me something. 'OK, Emma,' he finally said, 'I'll tell you if you promise not to tell anyone else, OK?' As I nodded, wondering what he could possibly have to tell me, he continued quietly, 'It's because I don't want my dad to get all obsessed with you like he did with another family in the last place we lived. There was a weird kid who went to my school who I got friendly with, and I accidently mentioned to Dad that he could bend spoons and stuff just by looking at them. His parents could do it too, and his grandparents, he said. Dad got all excited and wanted them on his show and he wouldn't leave the family alone after that. But they didn't want any fuss or to go on television and it all got really nasty at school when Dad wouldn't let it drop.

The Head took the other family's side and I got asked to leave. Dad was sorry about it because he knew I really liked that school, but he was more sorry that he didn't get that family to appear on his TV show.'

He paused. 'Anyway, if he carries on like this I can see the same thing happening here. He'll get into a similar thing with your family and our two families will end up hating each other. And all the other neighbours will take your side and they'll end up hating us too, and you'll hate me and everyone at my new school will hate me and eventually we'll have to move on yet again.'

I didn't say anything for a little bit after he'd told me all that. I was too busy thinking. And what I was thinking was that maybe there were even more difficult families to belong to than a super-weird one like mine.

'I'm sorry I haven't trusted you,' I finally said, giving Ziggy an apologetic smile. 'It's been quite scary having your family move next door, that's all.'

'I know.' He looked apologetic too. 'It's been pretty freaky for me as well, seeing your gnomes doing the weeding and those dolls throwing stuff at each other, and seeing your sister doing that stunt with the dustbin lorry just now. Not to mention Henry! I mean, that isn't exactly normal, is it?'

'I didn't say we were *normal*,' I clarified, 'just that we're not aliens, OK?'

'OK.' He paused. 'So what are you then?'

And that's when I decided the time had come to tell him the truth about us. After all, I was going to need his help and it wasn't as if he hadn't trusted me. I wasn't sure that my parents would approve, but I didn't see what else I could do.

'Wow, that's pretty cool!' he exclaimed when I'd finished talking. 'But I can see why you want to keep it a secret.' He looked thoughtful. 'Listen, you'll have to be really careful around my dad. He would expose you and Saffie with no hesitation if it meant his viewing figures went up.'

As he spoke the back door opened and his dad emerged.

'Here comes Dad for his daily trampoline workout. He really does use our trampoline to keep fit, you know. He didn't buy it *purely* to spy on any interesting neighbours!'

We watched Ziggy's dad jog down to the bottom of the garden and do a few stretches on the grass to limber up.

I remembered that Granny was meant to have sabotaged the trampoline by now. It was probably just as well that she hadn't, I thought, as we watched Mr Seaton haul his large body up to sit on the padded edge of the trampoline, which seemed to tilt a little under his weight.

I reckoned he must be *extremely* heavy, judging by the way the whole trampoline was sort of sinking down into the ground as he jumped on it. As we watched, the trampoline's legs seemed to be slowly disappearing into the earth. It was like watching somebody bouncing on a trampoline on top of quicksand! Ziggy's dad soon realized something was wrong and dismounted in a sort of rolling motion over the side. Unfortunately he landed with a splat on the muddy ground and rolled into the boggy hollow that the sinking trampoline was now stuck in.

Ziggy was running down the garden, calling, 'Are you all right, Dad?' while I followed at a slower pace.

'Do I look like I'm all right?' his father grunted as he crawled out covered in mud.

'Someone's done something to the ground under this trampoline. I don't know what exactly. Dug out a whole lot of soil from underneath it or something – and replaced the turf so it wouldn't be noticed. I should jolly well call the police!'

'What? To report the theft of some *earth*?' Ziggy sounded incredulous.

'I don't think the earth has been *stolen* exactly,' I said, pointing to a large pile of soil close to the hedge.

Ziggy's dad went to inspect it before turning back to glare at me. 'I don't suppose you already knew about this, did you?'

I shook my head, not really feeling like I was lying. After all, it wasn't as if Granny had told me what she'd done.

But he wasn't finished with his interrogation.

'And what about our missing garden shed? Do you know anything about *that*?'

In my panic I forgot all about 'V is for Vandals' and blurted out the first thing that came into my head. 'Maybe the wind blew it away?'

Mr Seaton narrowed his eyes. 'Really? I didn't notice a tornado but I guess one could have visited the garden while I was out!'

I gulped because I didn't like the way he was glaring at me. 'I think I'll go now,' I said. 'See you later, Ziggy.'

'See you, Emma. And thanks again for rescuing Henry!'

As I left I heard Ziggy's dad ask him in a suspicious voice, 'Now . . . tell me again . . . how exactly *did* those girls rescue that bear?'

CHAPTER 10

'Granny, what did you do?' I asked as soon as I got home. 'Ziggy's dad is furious. He thinks someone dug up the ground under his trampoline.'

'He's right.' Granny was smiling. 'It was my gnomes. I sent them over there to do what turned out to be rather a large spot of gardening. It took them all night. I did help them a little bit with the hose though. I thought it might be a nice touch to make the earth nice and boggy before they put the turf back on.'

'But, Granny, how did they do it without anyone seeing anything?'

'It was a night mission. My gnomes are quite expert at night missions. They looked like mini commandos climbing up one side of the hedge and down the other. We used your washing-line as a rope.'

'But, Granny, Ziggy's dad will just move his trampoline on to a firmer bit of ground and carry on using it,' I pointed out.

'He can move it and exercise on it as much as he likes, but if I catch him spying on us again I shall send the boys back over there. They're prepared to dig up his whole garden if necessary. He'll soon learn not to mess with this family!'

'I just hope you haven't made things worse, Mother,' Mum said as she came into the room.

'I doubt that,' Granny said. 'And the sooner he stops being such a nosy neighbour the better.'

'Where's Saffie?' I asked when I saw that she wasn't with our mother.

'I gave her dolls back to her and she's

playing with them in her room,' Mum replied.

I was puzzled. There was no noise coming from upstairs.

'I got her to make me a promise before I gave them back,' Mum added.

'What promise?' I asked.

'To teach them that if they don't play nicely with each other, then they won't get played with at all.'

Granny was tilting her head, cupping one hand behind her ear as if she was having a really good listen. 'Well . . .' she finally declared. 'I do believe that's done the trick, my dear.'

Mum nodded and gave a wry smile as she murmured, 'At least for now.'

As soon as Dad got home from work, Mum said she needed to talk to him in the kitchen. I knew she was going to tell him what had happened today with the bin lorry and how worried she was about Saffie using her power like that in public. And she was also going to tell him about my conversation with Ziggy and the fact that I had told Ziggy the truth about us. Mum had been furious when I'd let her know what I'd done. Granny was already in the kitchen, so I guessed she was planning on being in on their talk too.

The grown-ups had been shut up in the kitchen for some time when the doorbell rang. Saffie was in the living room watching television, so it was me who went to the door.

'Who is it?' I called out.

'Ziggy! Quick! Open the door! I don't want my mum to see me here!'

'*Why* mustn't she see you?' I asked as I let him inside.

'She's decided there's something about your family that's not quite right and she'd rather we kept our distance.' He grinned. 'Basically, she thinks you're all a bit weird, but not in an interesting or scientifically significant way.'

'Oh,' I said, wondering if I ought to feel insulted.

'Don't worry. It means she'll do her best to get Dad to drop *his* interest in you too,' Ziggy continued. 'She only likes him focusing on families who might be aliens, so she's trying to steer him back in that direction. She's written an advert to put in the paper. That's what I came to show you. Look!' He handed me a piece of paper with typing on it:

FREAKY FAMILIES, STEP RIGHT UP!

- Does anyone in your family have an unusual physical feature such as absent outer ears, a weirdly shaped head or an abnormal number of fingers or toes?
- Do any of your relatives practise an unusual or abnormal skill such as telepathy, fortune-telling or weather manipulation?
- Have you ever suspected, for any reason, that there could be an alien ancestor somewhere in your family's past?
- Would you and your family be willing to take part in an exciting TV talk show on the above topic?
- We are searching ONLY for families who genuinely suspect they may be descended from aliens.

As soon as I'd finished reading it I started to laugh. 'Who on earth would reply to this?'

'An alien who wants to be on TV maybe?' Ziggy replied with a grin.

'Yes, but a *real* family of aliens aren't going to expose themselves, are they?' I pointed out.

'Maybe not a full-on alien family who've just arrived from outer space,' Ziggy agreed. (And it was clear from his face that he didn't think such a thing existed.) 'But there are quite a few people out there who really *do* believe that one of their ancestors might have originated from another planet. And it's amazing how many people love the idea of being on television.'

Just then Saffie appeared in the hall. She was wearing her Supergirl outfit, but with red furry slippers on her feet instead of silver wellington boots.

'Can I borrow Henry, please?' she asked Ziggy. 'I'm going to have a teddy bear's tea-party tomorrow and I need lots of bears to be the guests. He'll have lots of fun!'

'Another time, OK, Saffie?' Ziggy said quickly. 'I think Henry's had all the excitement he can handle for one week.' He started to open the front door. 'I'd better go now, Emma.'

'OK. See you later.'

After he'd left I noticed that Granny had come out of the kitchen and was standing in the hall looking a little flushed. The kitchen door was open and Saffie immediately went through to see Mum and Dad.

'What's wrong, Granny?' I asked, because it was clear from her face that something was.

Granny answered in a low voice. 'I think I'd better warn you, Emma, that your father is rather upset with me. He made one Superman joke too many so I gave him a piece of my mind. I told him it was time he stopped poking fun at everything he doesn't understand and started to show some respect for our family's gift. I'm afraid he wasn't best pleased at being told off.'

Before I could respond, Mum called out that she'd made some drinks so we went through to the kitchen. Saffie was just about to go out into the garden, having swapped her red slippers for her silver wellies. Dad was sitting reading the paper. He smiled at me when I walked in but he didn't look at Granny.

'Who was that at the door, Emma?' Mum asked.

'Ziggy.' And I quickly told them about the advert Ziggy's mum was going to place in the paper.

'I do hope he doesn't tell his parents about us,' Mum said with a frown.

'He won't, Mum. He's on *our* side.' I attempted to reassure her.

'Well, I just hope Ziggy's mum knows what she's doing putting in an advert like that,' Dad said. 'I don't know about Godfrey but I know how *I'd* react if the freakiest families in the country started calling *me* up.'

'Don't be silly, Jim,' Mum responded impatiently. 'She'll use a mailbox address – not his phone number – and in any case, Godfrey *wants* to find freaky families. The freakier the better, as far as his TV ratings are concerned, I should think.'

'He might even discover some *genuine*

aliens among them,' Granny pointed out.

As both Dad and Mum gave her an incredulous look she said, 'Well, who knows how *our* family really came by our gift? Perhaps this story about an ancestor being struck by lightning *isn't* true. Perhaps we have an ancestor who was an alien instead!' She looked across at Dad and added, 'After all, Superman's powers came from another planet, did they not?'

Dad clearly wasn't sure if she was having another go at him or not. 'Look . . .' he said in a quiet voice. 'I'm sorry if I've offended you with all my superhero quips . . . You're right . . . it *is* disrespectful and I promise I'll try to keep my lip buttoned a bit more in future, OK?'

Granny looked surprised. 'Well, thank you, Jim, and *I'm* sorry for the many times

I've offended *you*. The trouble is, I find it hard to keep my opinions to myself when they concern the people I most care about.' Granny looked at him fondly as she added, 'You see, it's only because I think of you as a son that I feel I can speak to you as frankly as I do.'

Dad smiled and went a little bit pink. 'Well . . . that's good to know.'

Saffie was playing happily in the garden, running round the lawn with her arms outstretched, pretending to fly through the air like Supergirl.

'Now, Marsha . . . Jim . . . I do hope you aren't going to take what I'm about to say the wrong way . . .' Granny began – and I saw Mum in particular go from relaxed to tense in a matter of seconds. 'I doubt I am going to make any progress with Serafina as things are at the moment. She is a very different child to Emmeline and I am going to need to try a different approach.'

'What sort of approach?' Mum asked at once.

'Some more intensive training is needed, but I can't do that here, which is why I suggest that Saffie comes to stay with *me* for a while – on her own.'

'Oh, I don't think that's a very good idea,' Mum said at once. 'Perhaps if I were to come too . . .'

'Then the arrangement won't work,'

Granny said swiftly. 'Saffie needs to know that I'm in charge, and I won't be in charge if you're there.'

'Marsha, she's got a point,' Dad put in. 'Is it really such a bad idea to let Saffie go with her? After all, with Saffie gone, Godfrey's interest in us is bound to die down.'

But Mum still shook her head. 'I just don't like the idea of you and Serafina being alone together for that length of time, Mother. No offence, but I think somebody . . . well . . . *sensible* needs to be there as well.'

'Your father will be there,' Granny reminded her, looking more amused than offended by what Mum had said.

Mum sighed. 'You know very well that he wouldn't notice *what* the two of you were doing. I don't think his head would come out from behind his newspaper even if a hundred gnomes were rampaging about the place.'

Dad looked as if he was trying not to laugh as he quickly suggested, 'What about Emma? Emma is sensible.'

'Of course,' Granny responded. 'Emma is *very* sensible. I would be more than happy for her to come too if she would like it.'

'Oh, I'd *really* like it!' I said excitedly. 'Can I, Mum?'

I could tell that Mum was seriously considering the idea. 'It's true I'd feel a lot happier knowing that Emma was there to keep an eye on things. Though I don't want to give Emma *too* much responsibility. After all, *she's* just a child too.'

'Don't worry about Emma,' Granny said at once. 'I'll make sure she isn't allowed to be too grown-up and sensible while she's with me.'

Mum looked as if that hadn't been quite what she'd meant.

Dad looked at Granny in delight. 'So that's settled then. You're going to take both of them for the summer, and when they come back, Saffie will be . . .' He trailed off, looking out into the garden where my sister was spinning herself around on the spot with her arms outstretched, looking like the craziest little girl in the whole world.

'. . . Saffie will be a perfectly *normal* and *sensible* supergirl like me!' I finished for him.

And everyone – even Granny – laughed at that.

Also by Gwyneth Rees

The Magic Princess Dress

Read on for an extract!

It was Ava's mum who had suggested Ava take her fairytale book with her when she went to stay with her dad. Ava's mother had read to her from the book on many occasions and Ava always enjoyed listening to her animated voice bringing to life the entertaining – if unlikely – adventures of the various fairytale characters. Ava found the book extra-comforting now as she curled up on her bed at Dad's house to read her favourite story, about Cinderella. With any luck she would manage to forget for a little while that her mum was so far away.

Of all the storybook's heroines, Ava loved Cinderella the best. She wasn't sure why, but maybe it was because Cinderella seemed more believable at the start of *her* story than some of the other characters did at the starts of theirs. After all, in real life, nobody lived with seven dwarfs like Snow White – or

lived in a witch's tower, with hair as long as Rapunzel's. But losing your mother and having her replaced with a cruel stepmother and two horrible stepsisters was something Ava *could* imagine happening in real life. And because of that she always felt more drawn to Cinderella than to any of the other fairytale princesses. Of course the whole story became completely fanciful as soon as Cinderella's fairy godmother appeared and started waving her magic wand about, but by then Ava was always totally captivated. And time and time again she found herself being utterly charmed by Cinderella's magical transformation into the beautiful fairytale princess.

On this occasion, however, Ava found that she couldn't escape into the world of Cinderella as completely as she usually did. She couldn't seem to keep her mind on the story – and it wasn't just because she was missing Mum. The thing that was really bothering her was that Cindy, her cat, whom she had brought with her to Dad's house, had gone missing a few days earlier.

If only *I* had a fairy godmother who could magic Cindy back again, Ava thought, as she put down the book halfway through the story.

Her gaze fell on the little pile of CAT MISSING posters she had made using Dad's computer. There was a description of Cindy printed on each one, together with Ava's mobile-phone number and her dad's address in case anyone found her. Ava had already put up several posters on lamp posts in the streets around Dad's house.

Perhaps now would be a good time to go and see if she could put some up in the windows of the local village shops, she thought. After all, in *real* life there was no such thing as magic to help you out when you had a problem – and that meant that the only thing to do was to try and solve the problem for yourself.

She didn't bother to ask her dad – who was working in his study – if it was OK for her to go to the high street. Instead she wrote him a short note saying that she had gone out to look for Cindy, which she left on the kitchen table. It was Dad who had absent-mindedly left the back door open, letting Cindy escape into the garden. To make matters worse, Cindy's collar had fallen off – they had discovered it in the grass afterwards – so even if somebody had found her by now, they wouldn't know where she belonged. It had happened the day after Ava had arrived, and even though her dad obviously hadn't let Cindy out on purpose, Ava still felt angry with him. Both Ava and her mum had told him Cindy would have to be kept inside for the first few days to give her a chance to get used to her new environment – and he had promised he would be careful.

The trouble with Dad was that he never really listened to what you told him, thought Ava, as she left the house and set off towards the main street in the village. He was always thinking about something else, usually something to do with the books he

wrote – all about historical times.

Just as Ava was stopping to peer over
a wall into an overgrown front garden,
which was just the sort of hiding place
Cindy would like, her mobile phone started
ringing.

'Ava?' It was Dad and he sounded
worried. 'Where are you?'

'On that little side road that leads off
yours – the one that goes towards the high
street,' Ava told him. 'I thought I'd go and
see if any of the shops in the village will
put a poster of Cindy up in their windows.
Oh!' As she looked up she could see a small
corner shop a little further along the road.
'There's a shop on *this* street as well. Maybe I
can put one of my posters up in *its* window.'

There was a sharp intake of breath at the
other end.

7

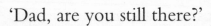

'Dad, are you still there?'

'Yes. Listen. I want you to come home right now.'

'No, Dad,' Ava protested, 'I need to stick these leaflets about Cindy in as many shop windows as I can.'

'Ava, you are not to go into the shop on that street. Do you hear me?'

'But why?' Ava was surprised. Generally her father didn't seem to care what she did as long as she kept out of his way when he was busy working.

'Never mind why.' Dad's voice sounded unusually heated now. 'Just do as I say. Come home now and I'll help you with those leaflets later.'

'OK, OK . . .' she grumbled, nearly adding, 'Keep your hair on!' which was what she often said to Mum when she got into a flap unnecessarily about something. But she stopped herself because she wasn't sure how her dad would react if she were to tease him like that. She knew her mum so much better than her dad. After all, until this summer she had spent the whole nine years of her life living with Mum, only seeing her father two or three times a year for the occasional weekend. As she had pointed out to Mum on the way here in the car, Dad felt more like a distant relative than a father.

'Which is why it's great that you're going to stay with him this summer,' her mother had replied.

'I still wish you weren't going away for a whole six weeks,' Ava had said, frowning. 'I'm really going to miss you.'

'And I'll miss you, darling, but this sailing trip is something I've always dreamed of

9

doing. And your dad misses you too, you know. He wants to spend this time with you.'

'No he doesn't,' Ava had said crossly. 'All he has time for are those stupid history books he writes.'

'Ava, that's not true,' Mum had replied gently.

But Ava hadn't been sure if she believed her.

Now, as she slipped the phone back into her pocket, Ava couldn't understand why her father was making such a fuss. She had kept walking as she talked to him and she was already right outside the little corner shop – which looked like it sold second-hand clothes.

On the wooden board above the window

the name of the shop – MARIETTA'S –
was painted in large curly lettering, and
the window display consisted of a solitary
mannequin wearing a fuzzy blonde wig and
an extremely faded, hideously unfashionable
blue sequinned dress. From what Ava could
see through the dirty windowpane, the

clothing inside wasn't much better.

Ava was about to leave when she spotted a little card taped to the glass door just below the 'open' sign.

Printed on the card in large clear lettering were the words: *FEMALE TABBY CAT FOUND. ENQUIRE WITHIN.*

'Cindy!' Ava gasped, and totally forgetting everything else, she tried the door handle. The door opened at once setting off a little bell inside the shop.

Suddenly feeling sick in case the cat that had been found *wasn't* Cindy, Ava tried to stay calm as she looked around. She was standing in the small front section of the shop, which had a round clothes rack in the centre, full of the sort of second-hand clothes typically found in charity shops. Along one wall another rack was partly filled with dusty-looking old coats and jackets. The shop was half empty of stock, and what there was looked like it had been there for a very long time.

Oh, please let Cindy be here, Ava thought desperately.

In the centre of the back wall was a small archway, which presumably led through to the next room, but Ava wasn't sure if that room was also part of the shop or whether it was private. A multicoloured beaded curtain hung in the arch, preventing Ava from seeing through.

Ava was just wondering whether to call out to let whoever ran the shop know that she was there, when the curtain moved and a smiling young woman appeared.

The woman was slim with pale skin, green eyes and long, wavy, copper-coloured

13

hair that fell to her waist. She looked ten years or so younger than Ava's parents – in her late twenties maybe – and she wore a long flowing orange dress with big red flowers on it. Her sandals were also orange and she had a stunning necklace made of amber-coloured beads.

'Welcome,' the woman said, smiling at Ava cheerfully. 'I am Marietta. How can I help you?'

'I just read the notice in your window,' Ava mumbled shyly. 'I've

14

lost my cat and I think you might have found her.'

'Really?' The young woman was beaming now. 'What's your name?'

'Ava.'

'Ava! Such a pretty name! How long ago did you lose your cat, Ava?'

'It's been four days. My dad accidently let her out into the garden. I only just came to stay with him and I think she must have got lost. She's a tabby cat with a white bit on her front paw. Does the one you found have a white bit on her front paw?'

'Yes, I think she does.' And Marietta turned and disappeared through the beaded curtain without saying whether Ava should follow her or not.

Feeling curious, Ava followed as far as the archway before hesitating. She could hear

Marietta calling, 'Come here, puss! Oh . . . where *are* you? You were here a minute ago!'

'Maybe she'll come if *I* call her!' Ava suggested through the curtain.

'Of course! Come and help me look! I know she's here somewhere.'

So Ava pushed through the beaded partition and found herself in a very different room indeed.

'Wow!' she burst out, hardly able to believe that she was still in the same shop.

Marietta laughed. 'Do you like it?' she said. As Ava nodded enthusiastically Marietta added, 'I only let *special* customers get to see my *real* shop! First let's find your cat – then I'll show you round!'